THE
MIDNIGHT
FRIDGE

By
Bruce Glassman

Illustrated by
Brian Lies

a **blackbirch** picturebook
woodbridge, connecticut

For Nathan and Emma
—BG

For Tom and Anu Chittenden
—BL

Published by Blackbirch Press, Inc.
260 Amity Road
Woodbridge, CT 06525

web site: http://www.blackbirch.com
email: staff@blackbirch.com

©1998 by Blackbirch Press, Inc.
First Edition

Printed in the United States of America

10 9 8 7 6 5 4 3 2 1

Library of Congress Cataloging-in-Publication Data

Glassman, Bruce.
    The midnight fridge / by Bruce Glassman : illustrated by Brian Lies
        p.   cm.
    "A Blackbirch picture book."
    Summary: Late one night, all the foods in the refrigerator start arguing about which one is the best.
    Summary: Stories in rhyme.
    ISBN 1-56711-801-1 (alk. paper)   ISBN 1-56711-805-4 (trade jacketed)
    [1. Food—Fiction.] I. Lies, Brian, ill. II. Title.
PZ8.3.G4264In   1998
[E]—dc21
                                                                            97-38431
                                                                            CIP
    3 9082 07251 9518   AC

It was inside the fridge
One dark midnight,
When cream cheese helped pickle
To turn on the light.

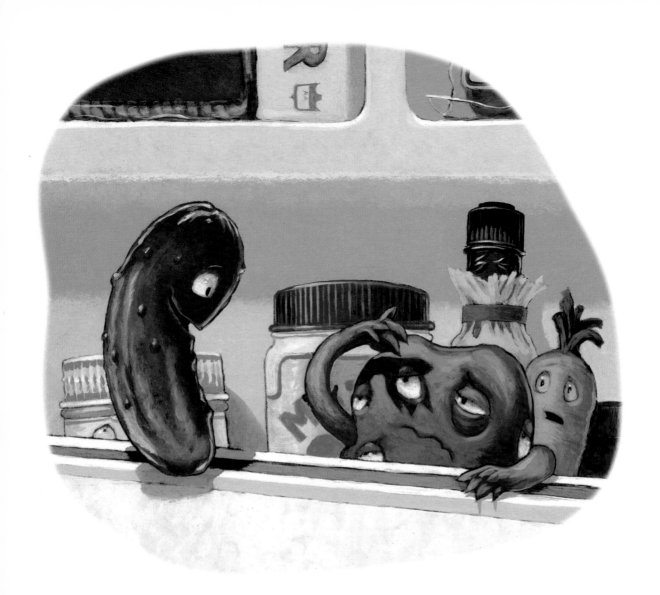

As the other foods woke
With alarm and surprise,
There were stretches and yawns
And even some cries.

Hot pepper and mustard
Both took the floor
And reminded all gathered
What this wake-up was for.

"Time to get up now,
Tonight's the contest
When all the foods gather
To see who's the best."

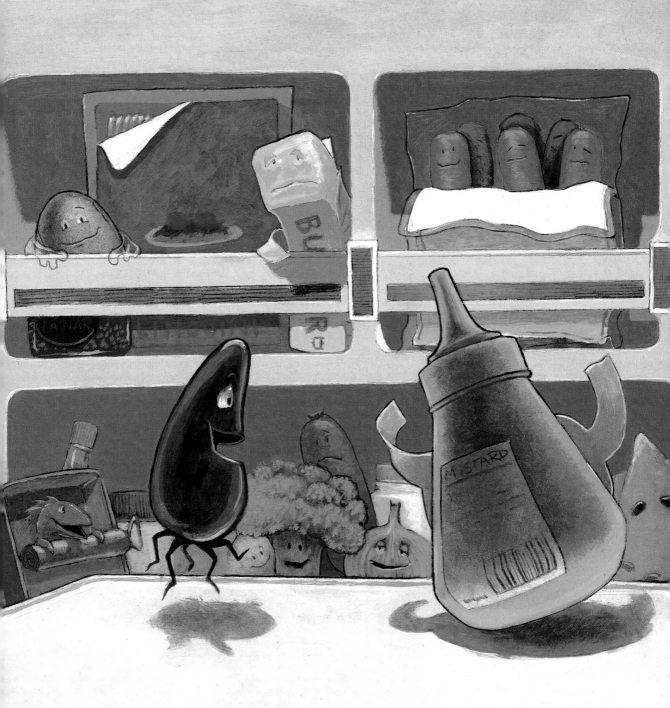

The lime Jell-O jiggled,
The squashes all squealed,
And orange and grapefruit
Both jumped as they peeled.

Excitement soon built
As the foods took their places;
Tater's eyes were aglow
As he went through his paces.

"I am the best food
And deserve the first prize;
You can hash me and mash me
And even make fries."

"But you have no flavor
Without me, you know,"
The butter was blabbing
As part of his show.

"Quiet down butter,"
Egg said with a groan.
"You're just a melt-in,
You can't stand on your own."

"I am the top food,"
Egg boasted with pride.
"I can be scrambled
Or flipped and then fried."

"You need me in baking,
In pancakes and pies;
I am most egg-cellent
And deserve the top prize."

"Now wait just a minute,"
The hot dogs chimed in.
"Mustard and relish say
Frankfurts should win.

"Kids like us the best
Tucked into our rolls;
More than their oatmeal
Or rice in their bowls."

Now spinach got mad,
Tomato juice boiled;
Rotini the pasta
Completely uncoiled.

The grapes started whining,
Apple juice was upset;
Which got the zucchini
And carrots all wet.

When onions and garlic
Got together to curse,
The milk and the yogurt
Took a turn for the worse.

Then all of a sudden
In the blink of an eye,
A battle erupted;
Food started to fly.

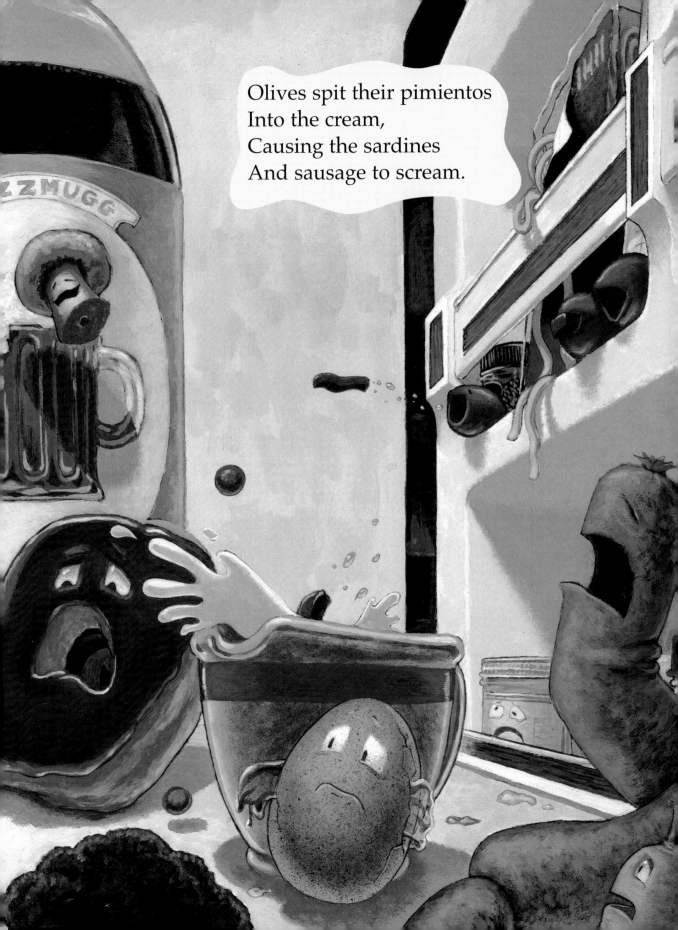

Mayo was flung
By some crass cauliflower,
Making lemons and limes
Turn even more sour.

From out of the fray
Hero sandwich stood tall,
And halted the fighting
With his bold and brave call.

"STOP!" he cried.

Then he spoke.

"No food is THE BEST;
Each has its own place,
And each on its own
Brings a smile to one's face."

"I also need lettuce
And onions and cheese
To make me a hero,
A sandwich to please."

Peanut butter hugged jelly
And bacon kissed egg;
Mayo nudged chicken
And gave a pat on the leg.

Peace was restored
As milk dimmed the light;
So the foods could chill out
For the rest of the night.